OPHELIA HOUSE

LUNCH AT LANGLEY'S

ORIGINAL ARTWORK

ANDREW L. WILLIS

CREATED AND WRITTEN

CARLTON L. SAMPSON

COVER DESIGN, BALLOONS, PAGE LAYOUT

Palanquin

THE LANGLEY RESIDENCE

© 2015 CARLTON L. SAMPSON • ANDREW L. WILLIS

*PO LYN LEE "OPHELIA HOUSE" EPISODE 3 "LADY LIBERTY" PAGE 19.

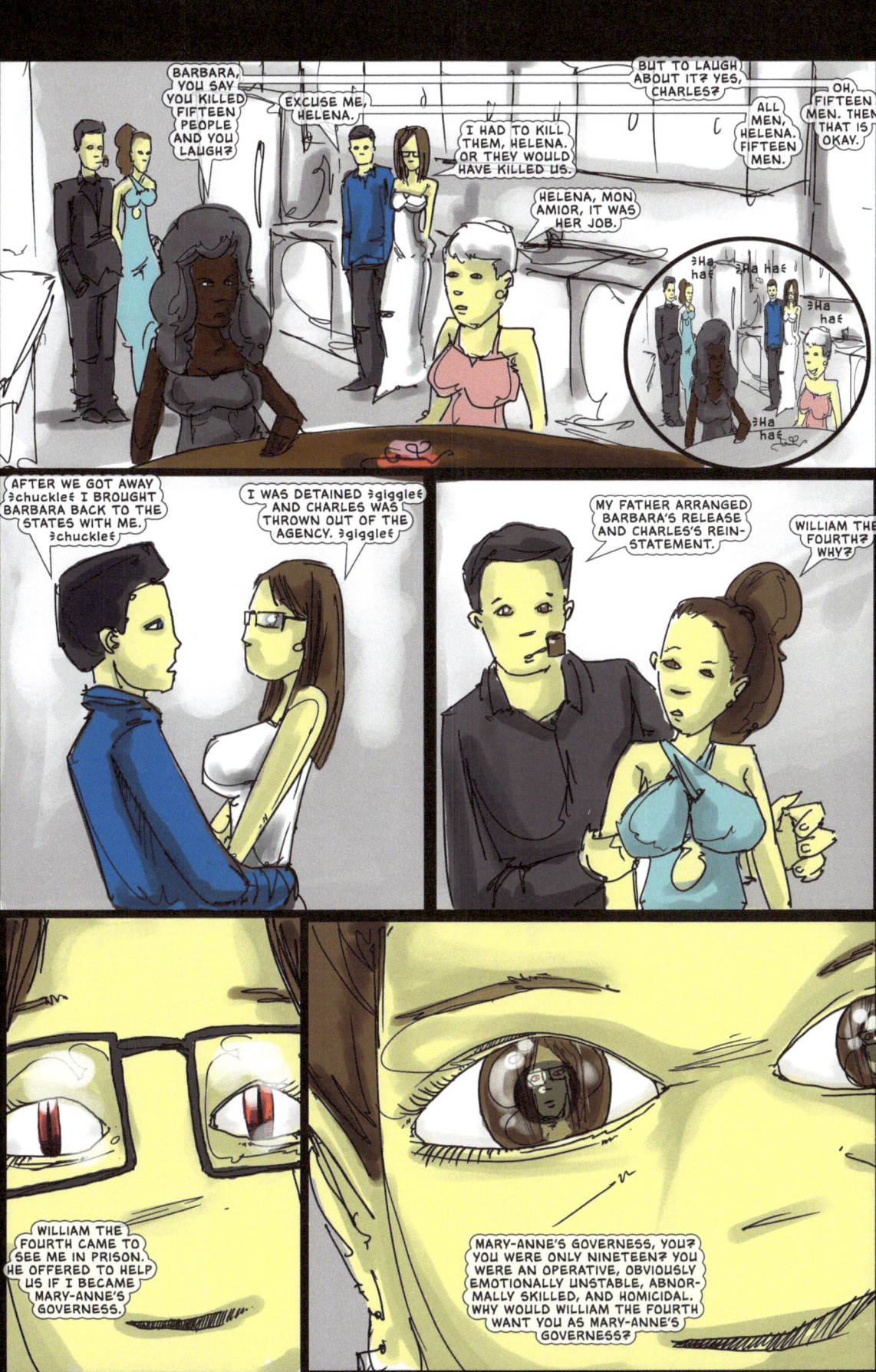

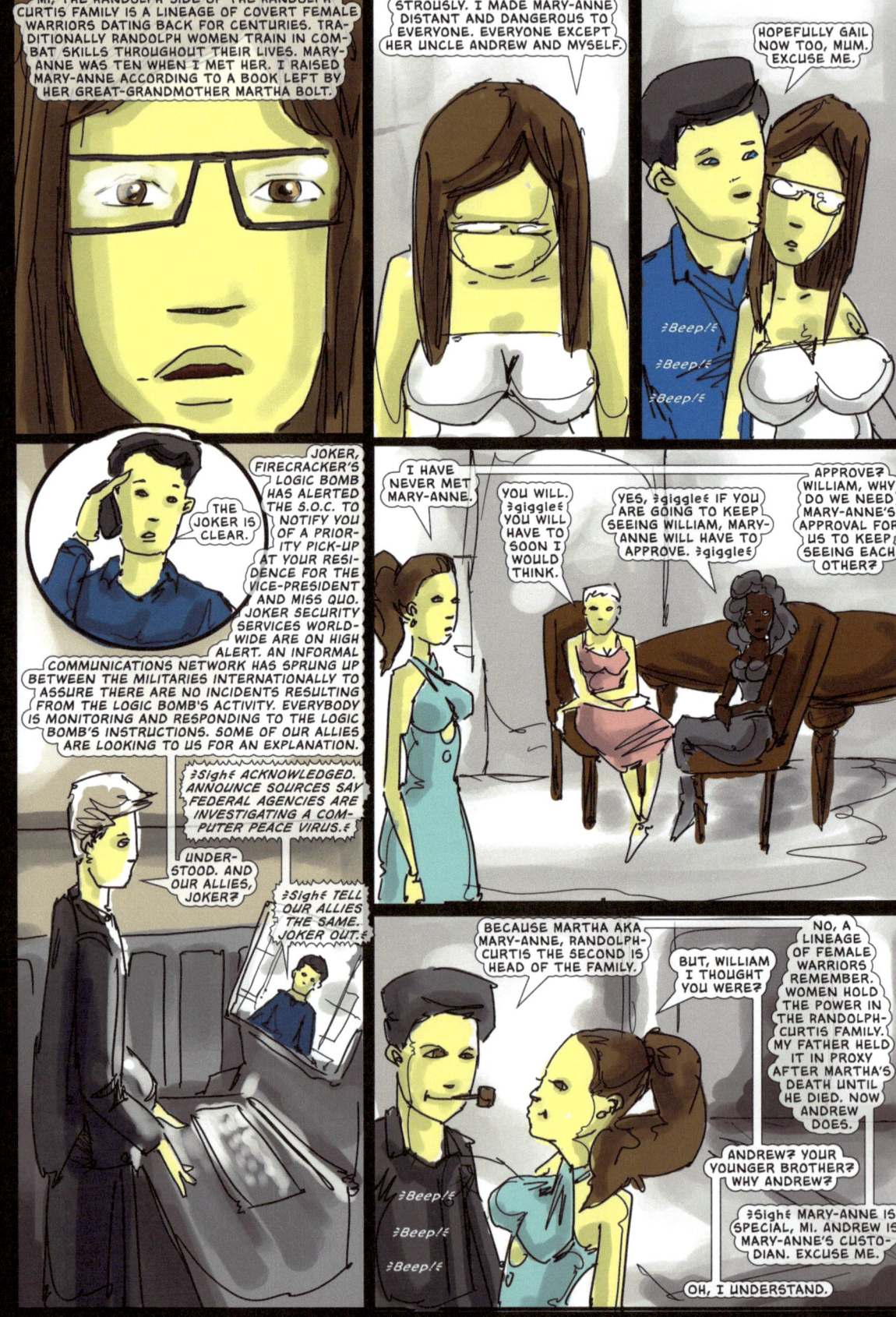

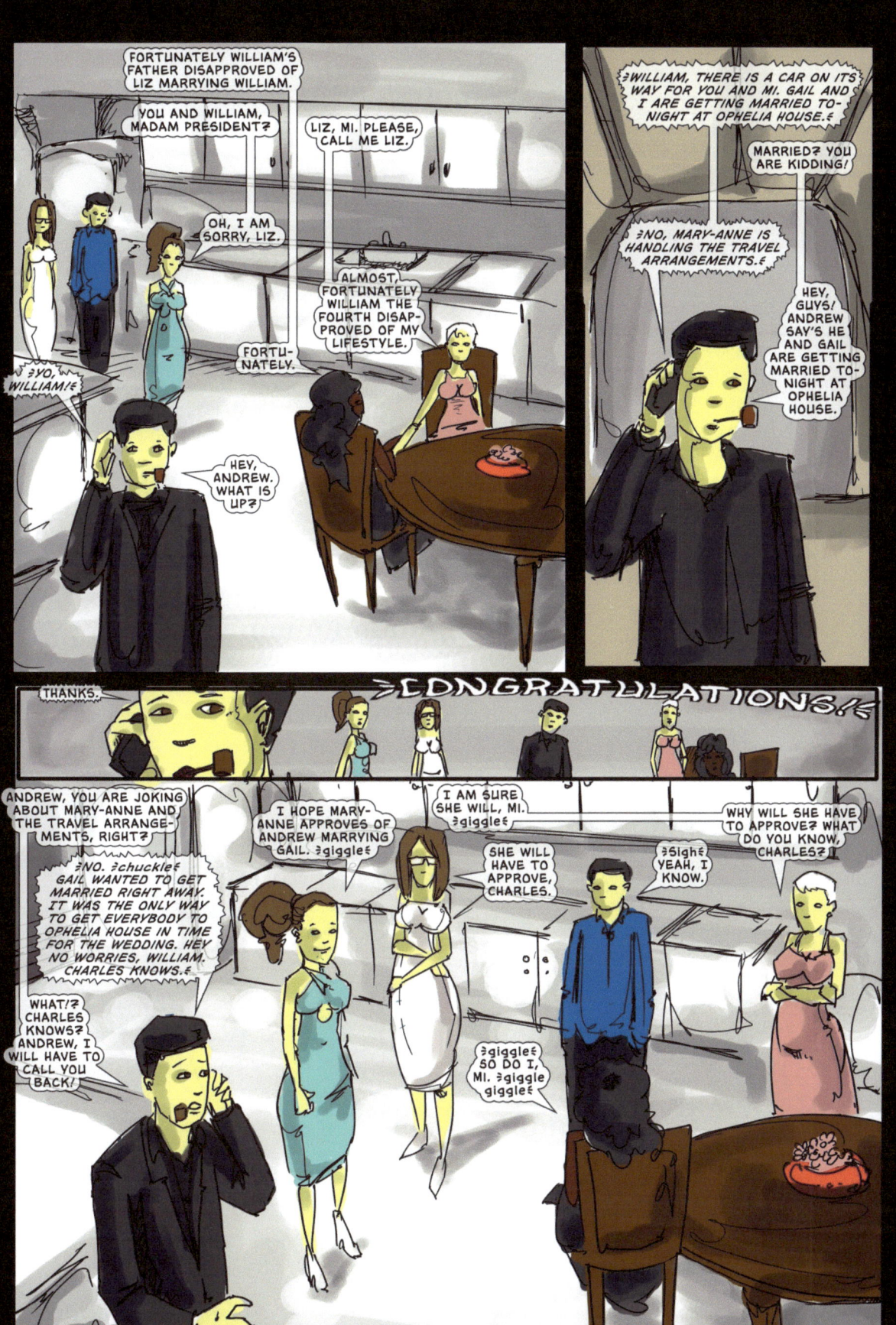

*INTERNAL SECURITY DEPARTMENT, SINGAPORE'S DOMESTIC INTELLIGENCE AGENCY.

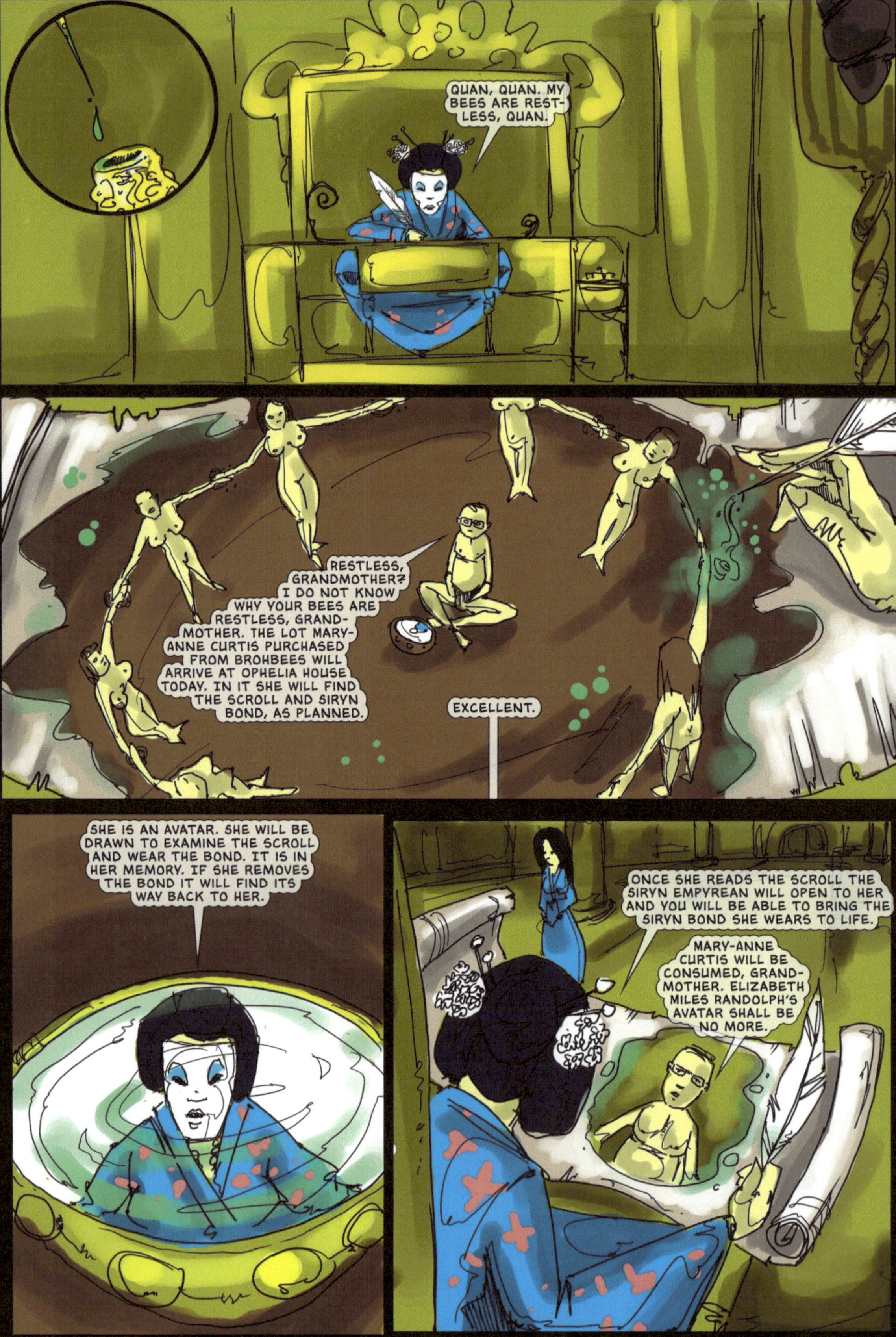

- 18 -

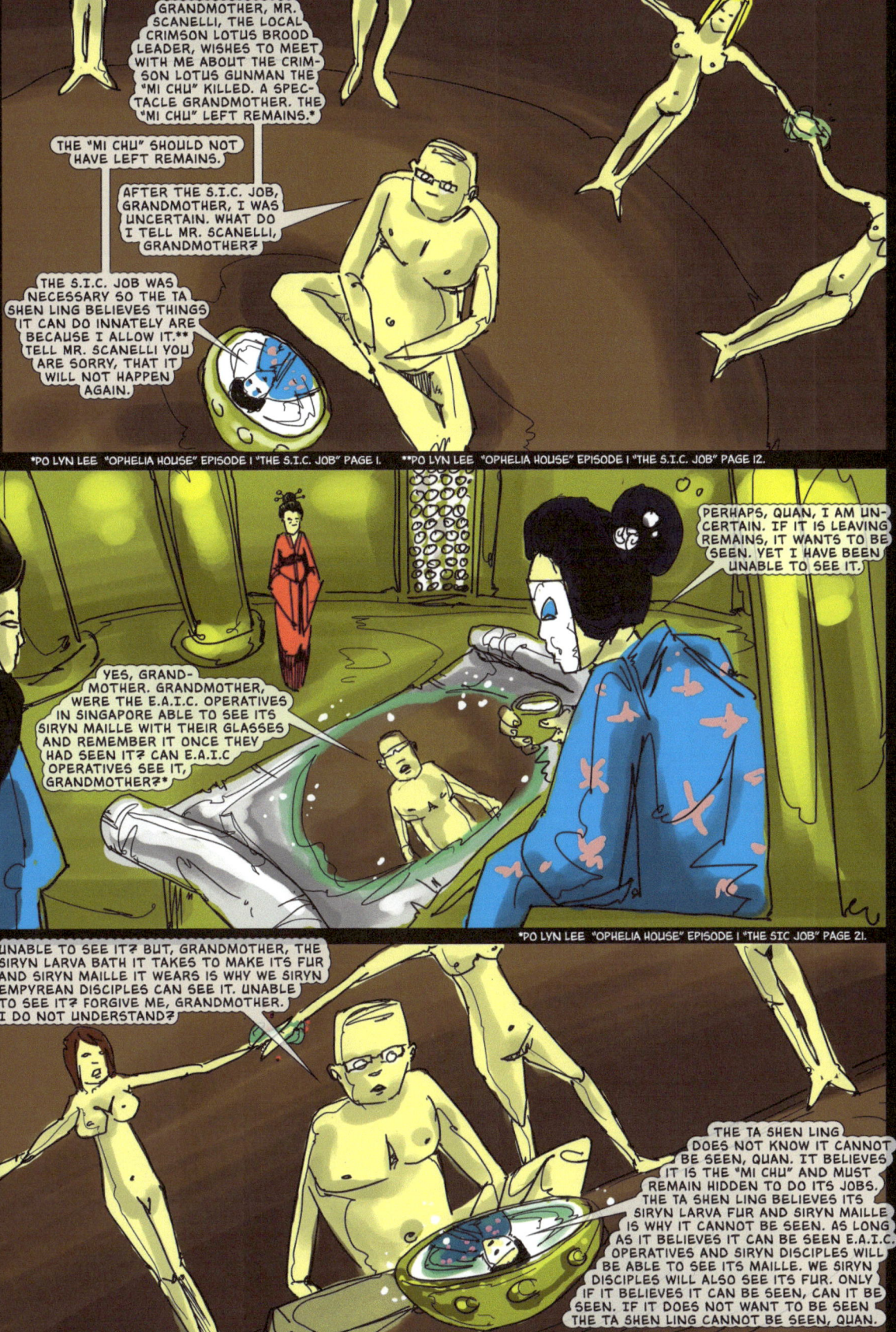

GRANDMOTHER, MR. SCANELLI, THE LOCAL CRIMSON LOTUS BROOD LEADER, WISHES TO MEET WITH ME ABOUT THE CRIMSON LOTUS GUNMAN THE "MI CHU" KILLED. A SPECTACLE GRANDMOTHER. THE "MI CHU" LEFT REMAINS.*

THE "MI CHU" SHOULD NOT HAVE LEFT REMAINS.

AFTER THE S.I.C. JOB, GRANDMOTHER, I WAS UNCERTAIN. WHAT DO I TELL MR. SCANELLI, GRANDMOTHER?

THE S.I.C. JOB WAS NECESSARY SO THE TA SHEN LING BELIEVES THINGS IT CAN DO INNATELY ARE BECAUSE I ALLOW IT.** TELL MR. SCANELLI YOU ARE SORRY, THAT IT WILL NOT HAPPEN AGAIN.

*PO LYN LEE "OPHELIA HOUSE" EPISODE I "THE S.I.C. JOB" PAGE I.   **PO LYN LEE "OPHELIA HOUSE" EPISODE I "THE S.I.C. JOB" PAGE 12.

PERHAPS, QUAN, I AM UNCERTAIN. IF IT IS LEAVING REMAINS, IT WANTS TO BE SEEN. YET I HAVE BEEN UNABLE TO SEE IT.

YES, GRANDMOTHER. GRANDMOTHER, WERE THE E.A.I.C. OPERATIVES IN SINGAPORE ABLE TO SEE ITS SIRYN MAILLE WITH THEIR GLASSES AND REMEMBER IT ONCE THEY HAD SEEN IT? CAN E.A.I.C OPERATIVES SEE IT, GRANDMOTHER?*

*PO LYN LEE "OPHELIA HOUSE" EPISODE I "THE SIC JOB" PAGE 21.

UNABLE TO SEE IT? BUT, GRANDMOTHER, THE SIRYN LARVA BATH IT TAKES TO MAKE ITS FUR AND SIRYN MAILLE IT WEARS IS WHY WE SIRYN EMPYREAN DISCIPLES CAN SEE IT. UNABLE TO SEE IT? FORGIVE ME, GRANDMOTHER. I DO NOT UNDERSTAND?

THE TA SHEN LING DOES NOT KNOW IT CANNOT BE SEEN, QUAN. IT BELIEVES IT IS THE "MI CHU" AND MUST REMAIN HIDDEN TO DO ITS JOBS. THE TA SHEN LING BELIEVES ITS SIRYN LARVA FUR AND SIRYN MAILLE IS WHY IT CANNOT BE SEEN. AS LONG AS IT BELIEVES IT CAN BE SEEN E.A.I.C. OPERATIVES AND SIRYN DISCIPLES WILL BE ABLE TO SEE ITS MAILLE. WE SIRYN DISCIPLES WILL ALSO SEE ITS FUR. ONLY IF IT BELIEVES IT CAN BE SEEN, CAN IT BE SEEN. IF IT DOES NOT WANT TO BE SEEN THE TA SHEN LING CANNOT BE SEEN, QUAN.

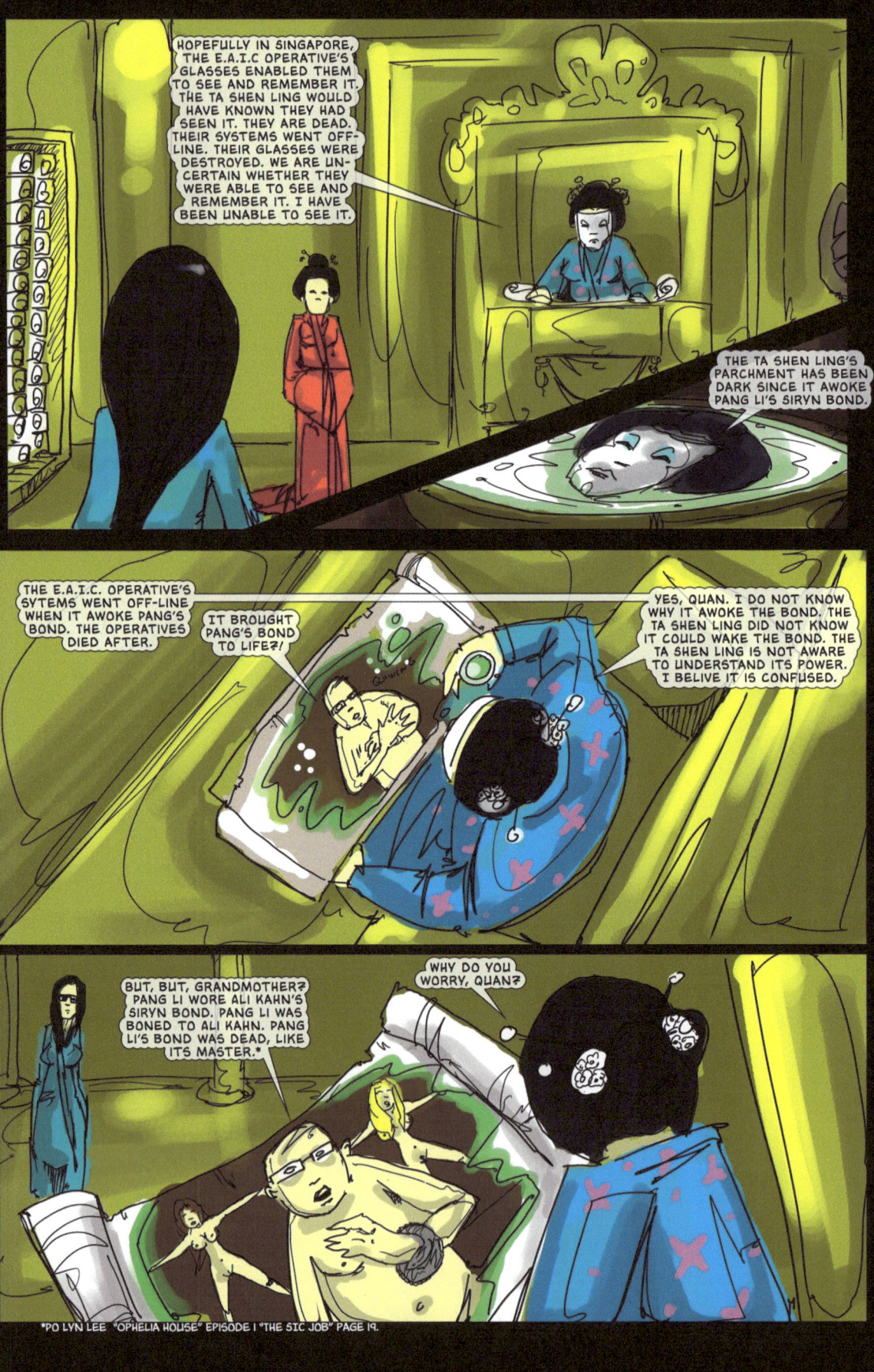

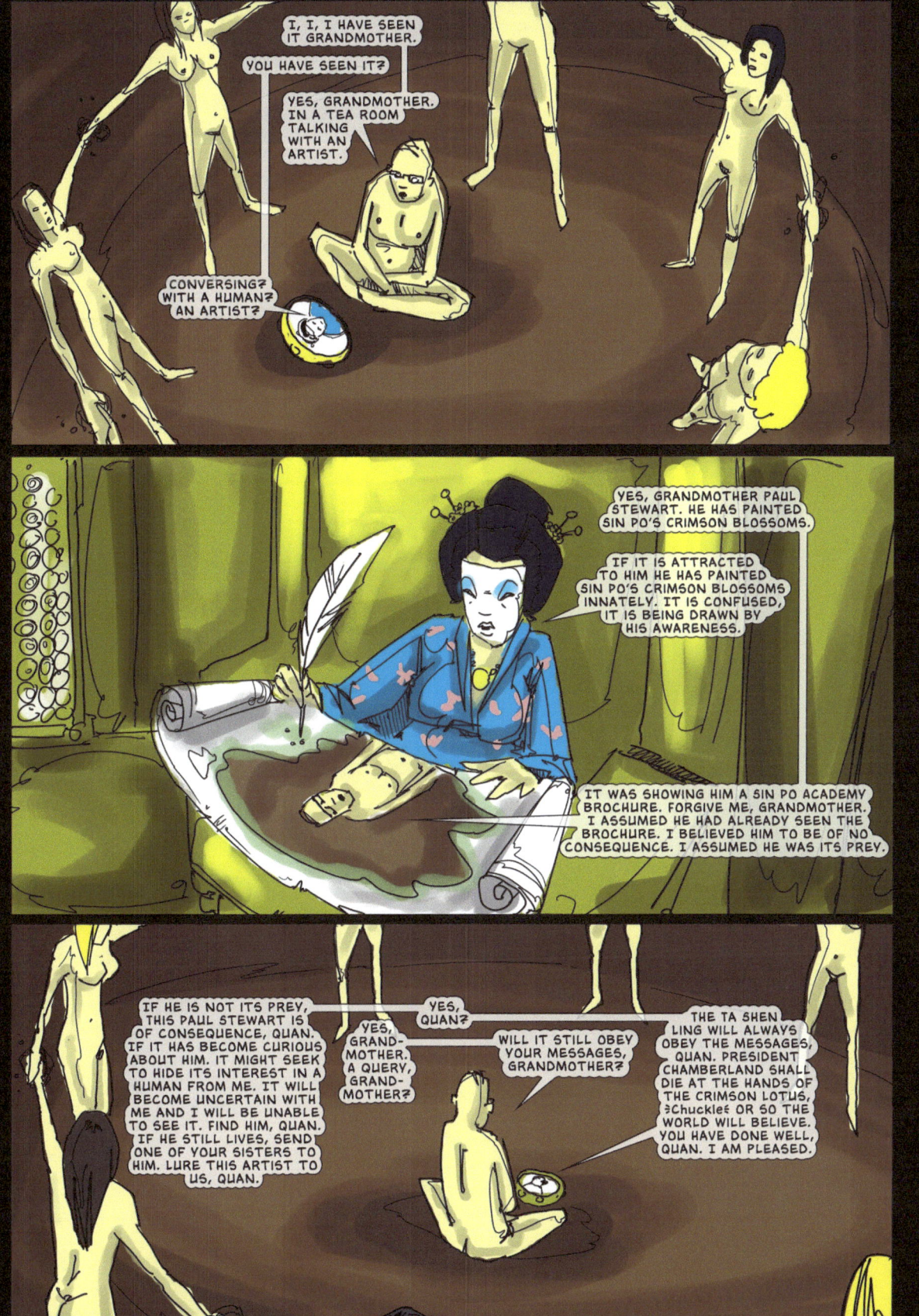

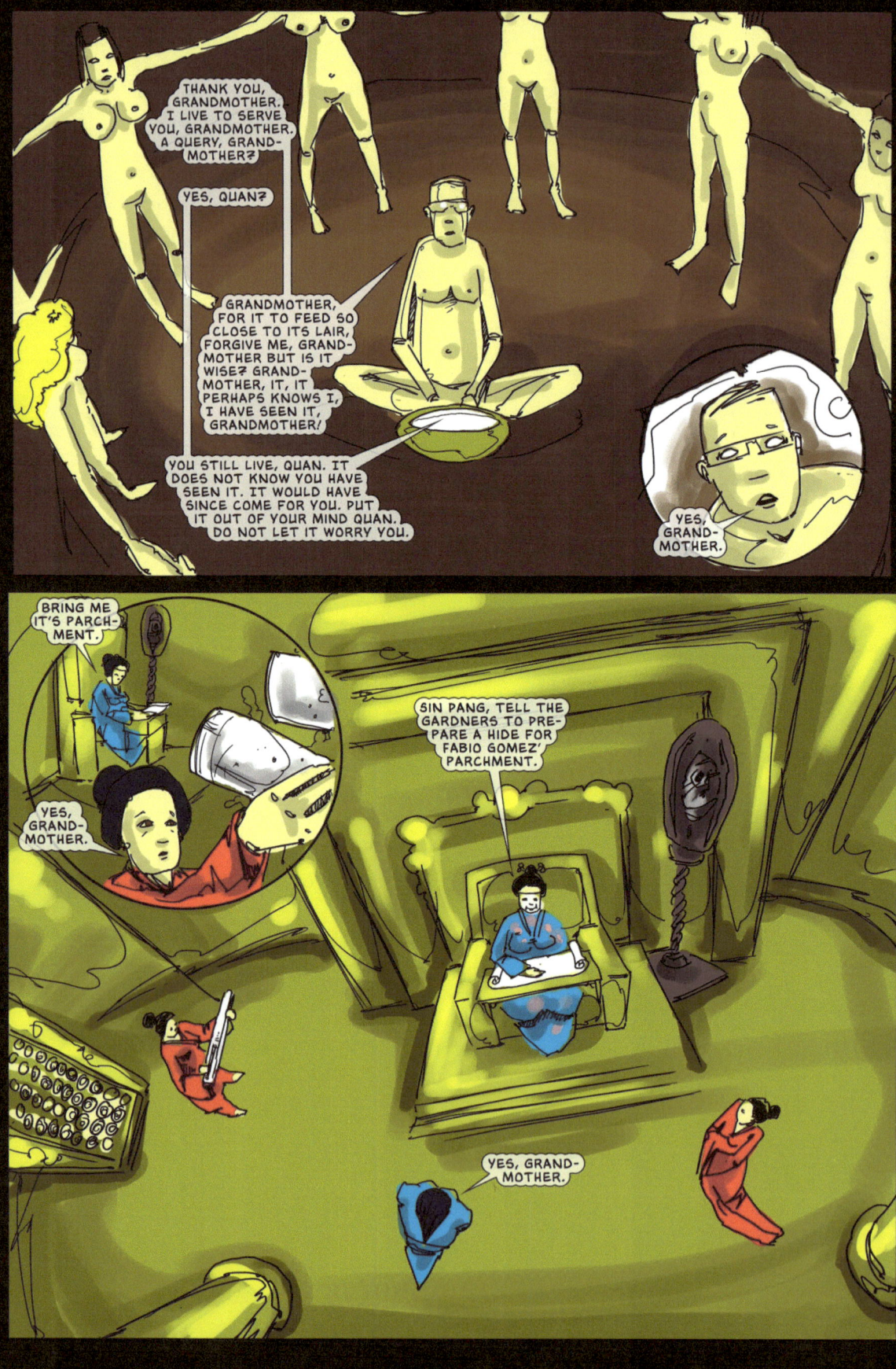

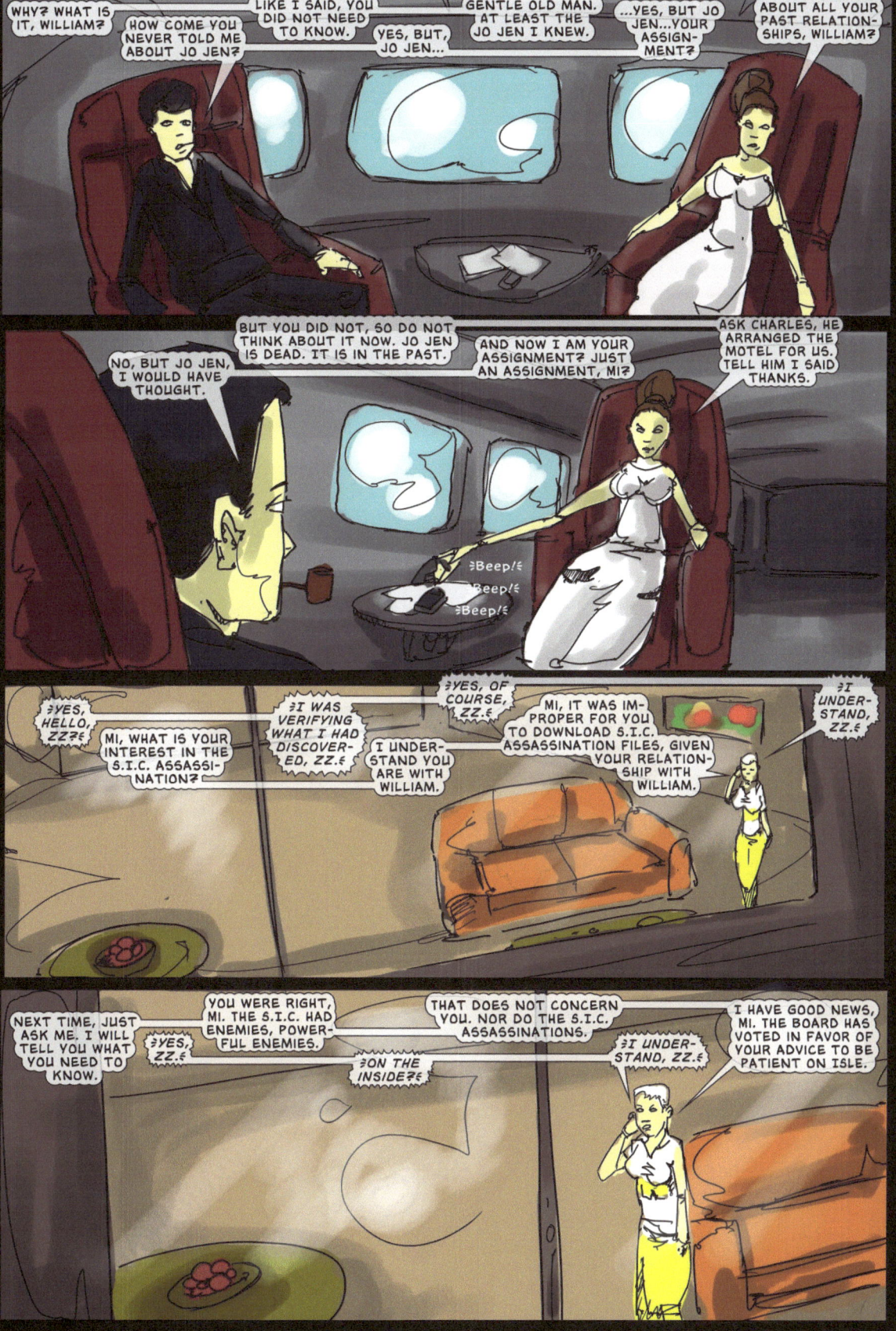

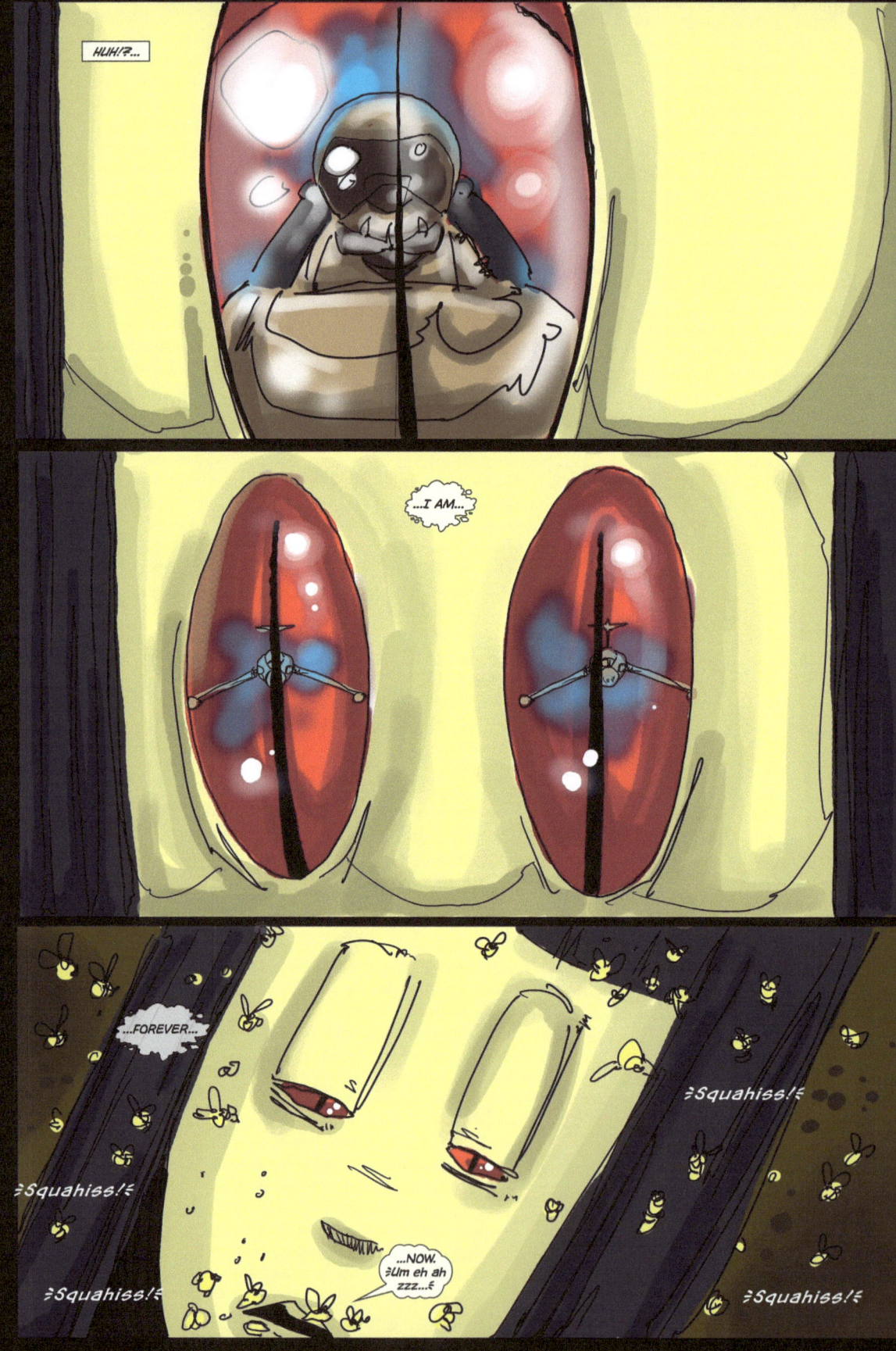

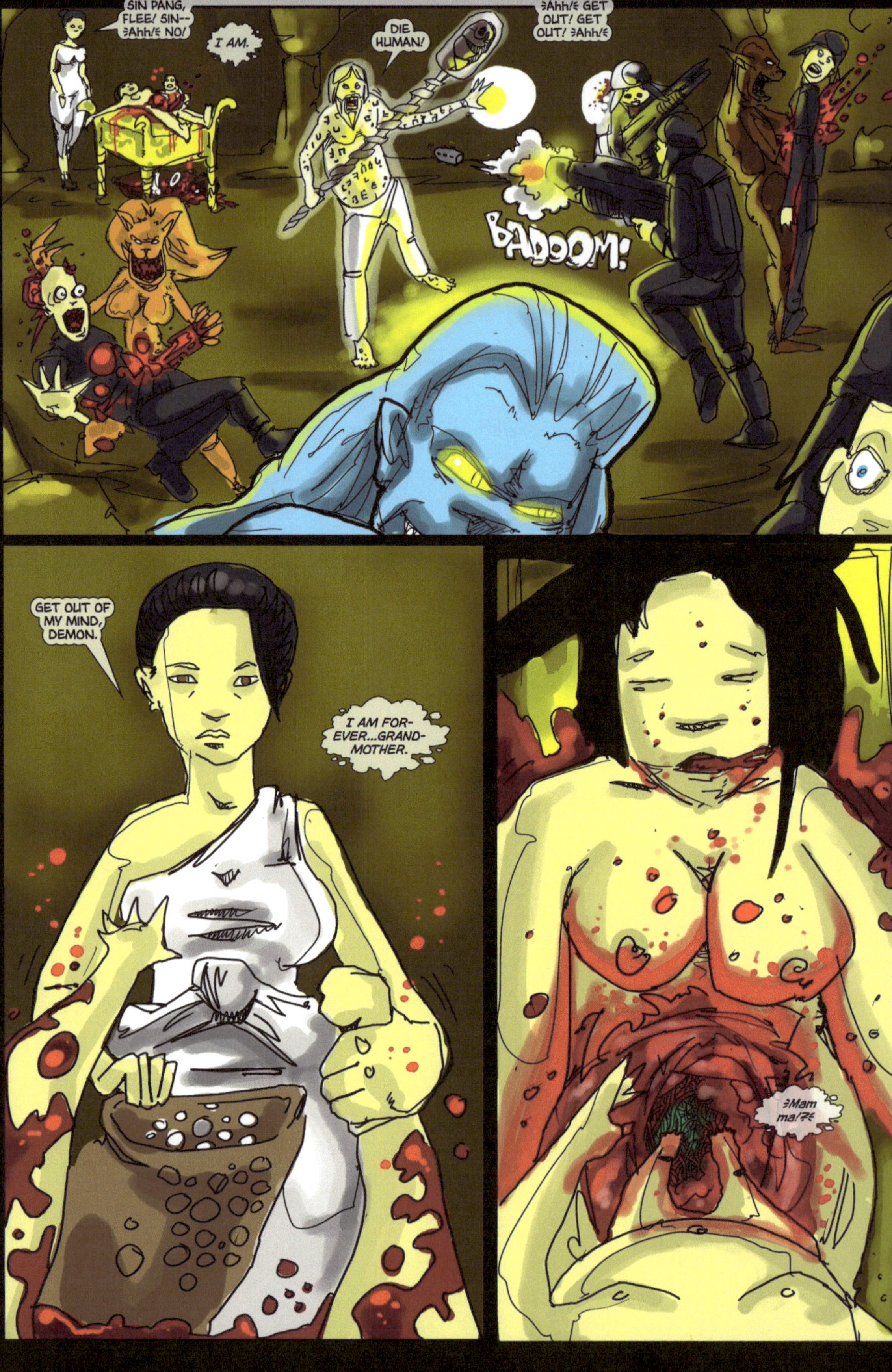

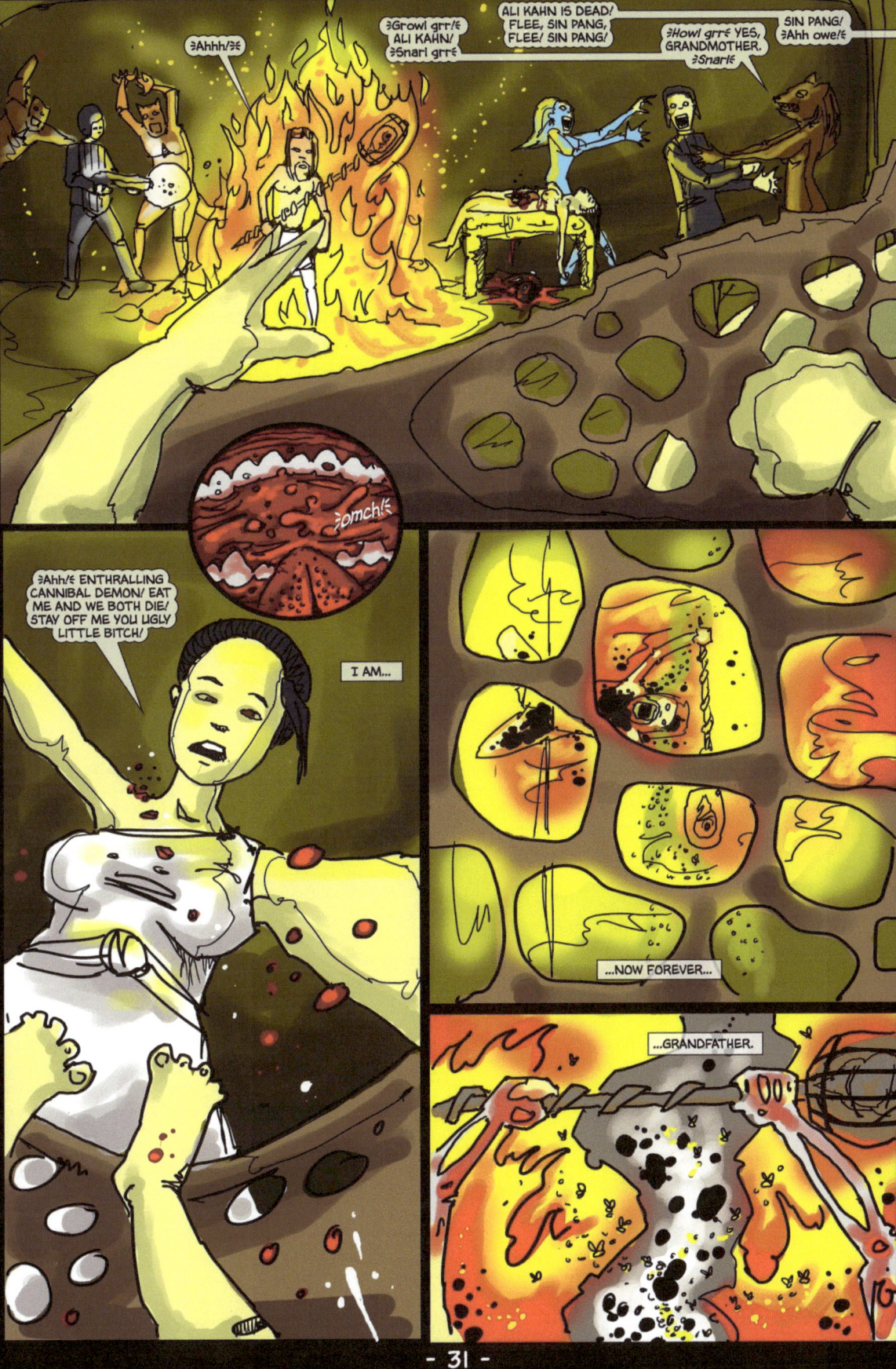

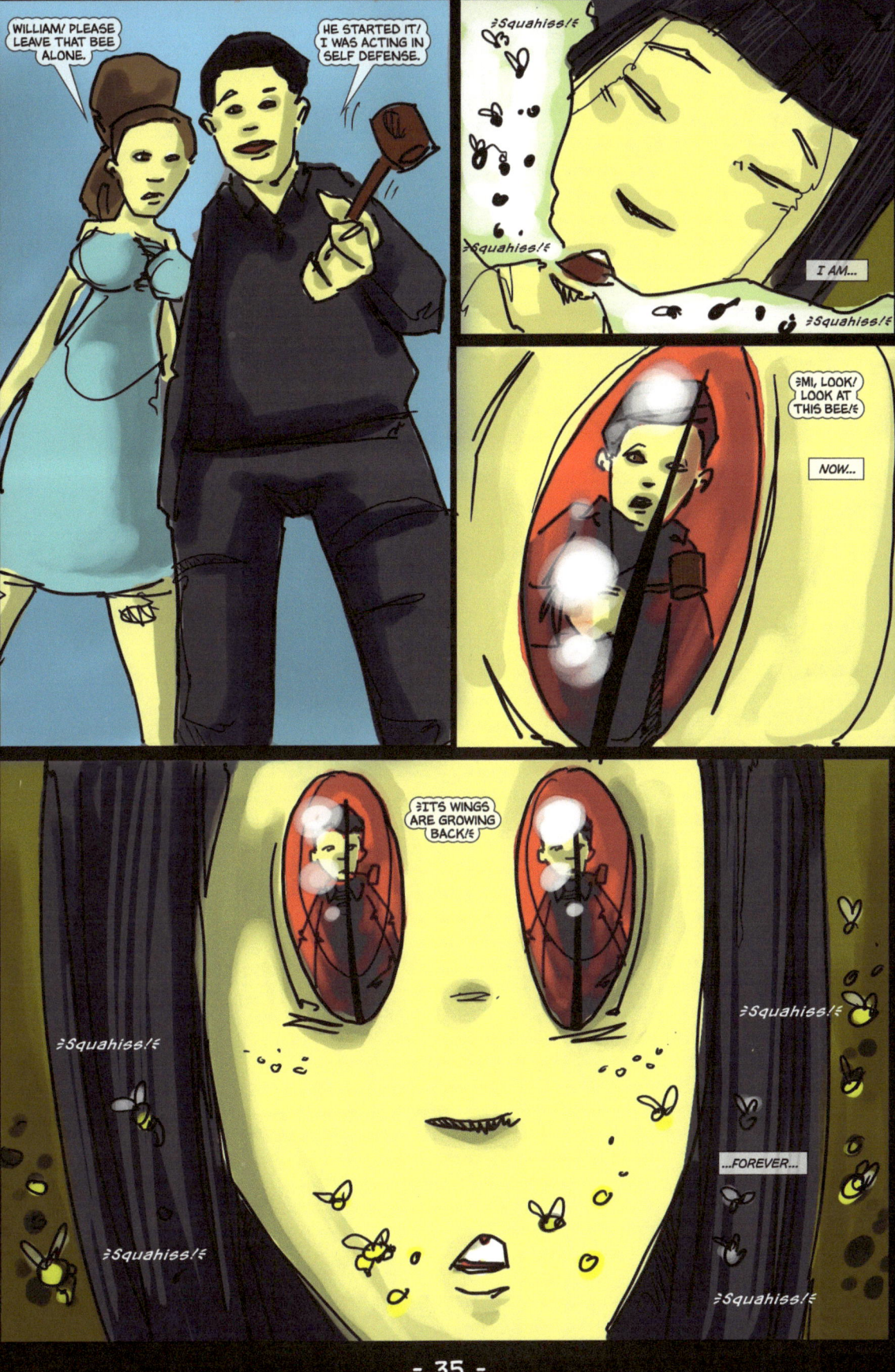

*PO LYN LEE "OPHELIA HOUSE" EPISODE 4 "FIRST FRIDAY" PAGE 39.

GRANDMOTHER SEE ME AND MR RON.

GRANDMOTHER SEE ME IN MR. PAUL'S LAIR. SEE MY FRIENDS.

GRANDMOTHER WILL PUNISH ME.

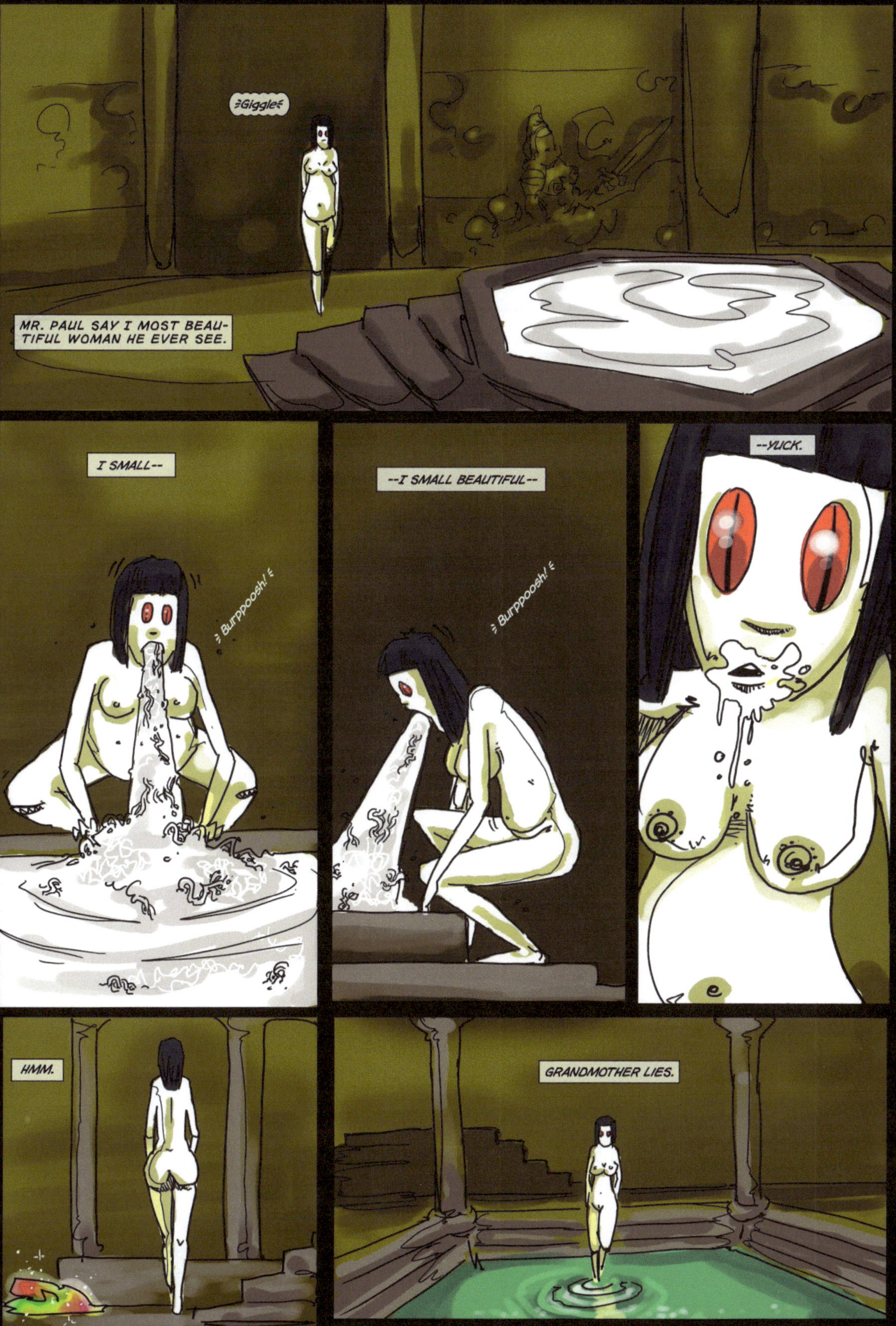

≈Giggle≈

MR. PAUL SAY I MOST BEAU-
TIFUL WOMAN HE EVER SEE.

I SMALL--

≈ Burppoosh! ≈

--I SMALL BEAUTIFUL--

≈ Burppoosh! ≈

--YUCK.

HMM.

GRANDMOTHER LIES.

*PO LYN LEE "OPHELIA HOUSE" EPISODE I "THE S.I.C. JOB" PAGE 20-21.

GRANDMOTHER SAY TAKE BATH.
SIGH.
MR. PAUL LIKE MY FUR.
MR. PAUL'S CARDS NICE. MR. PAUL TAKE THEM FROM MR. RUPERT AND GIVE THEM TO ME SPECIAL.
Sigh giggle giggle giggle giggle
I TOUCH MR. PAUL LIKE IN HIS MESSAGE BUT MR. PAUL NOT KNOW HOW?

PO LYN LEE
OPHELIA HOUSE
NEXT ISSUE

"PRIVATE WEDDING"

SOMEONE COMES WITH A MESSAGE AND IT
IS CLEAR. THE CRIMSON LOTUS DOES NOT
SEE THINGS FROM QUAN LO'S POINT OF VIEW.
MI QUO FINALLY GETS AN AUDIENCE WITH
MARTHA RANDOLPH CURTIS THE SECOND
BUT IS UPSTAGED BY THE PRESIDENT'S
ARRIVAL. IN THE FULL MOON LIGHT MUM
INSIST THERE IS MORE TO PO THAN MEETS
THE EYE.

CARLTON L. SAMPSON

POET, GRAPHIC NOVELL AUTHOR
CARLTON@POLYNLEE.COM
OTHER WORK AVAILABLE AT:
WWW.PHASCISTCLOWNS.COM

ANDREW L. WILLIS

AKA, THIOBIS THE ARTIST
FINE ART, SCULPTURE, ANIMATION,
MUSIC, AND WRITTEN.
ANDREW@POLYNLEE.COM
OTHER WORK AVAILABLE AT:
WWW.WAOOBAKEARTWORK.COM

COPY EDITOR "THE MUSE"

THIS IS A WORK OF FICTION. NAMES,
CHARACTERS, BUSINESSES, PLACES, EVENTS AND
INCIDENTS ARE EITHER THE PRODUCTS OF THE
AUTHOR'S IMAGINATION OR USED IN A
FICTITIOUS MANNER. ANY RESEMBLANCE
TO ACTUAL PERSONS, LIVING OR DEAD, OR
ACTUAL EVENTS IS PURELY COINCIDENTAL.

OPHELIA HOUSE
GYMNASIUM

SOMEONE COMES WITH A MESSAGE AND IT IS CLEAR. THE CRIMSON LOTUS
DOES NOT SEE THINGS FROM QUAN LO'S POINT OF VIEW. MI QUO FINALLY
GETS AN AUDIENCE WITH MARTHA RANDOLPH CURTIS THE SECOND BUT
IS UPSTAGED BY THE PRESIDENT'S ARRIVAL. IN THE FULL MOON LIGHT
MUM INSIST THERE IS MORE TO PO THAN MEETS THE EYE.

NEXT ISSUE

WWW.POLYNLEE.COM

© 2015 CARLTON L. SAMPSON • ANDREW L. WILLIS

www.ingramcontent.com/pod-product-compliance
Lightning Source LLC
Chambersburg PA
CBHW041537240626
47164CB00002B/47